ME & MY MOM

Other Books by Marianne Hauser

Shadow Play in India
Dark Dominion
The Choir Invisible
A Lesson in Music
The Talking Room
The Memoirs of the Late Mr. Ashley:
An American Comedy
Prince Ishmael

ME *&* MY MOM

Marianne Hauser

SUN &
MOON

CLASSICS

36

LOS ANGELES
SUN & MOON PRESS
1993

Sun & Moon Press
A Program of The Contemporary Arts Educational Project, Inc.
a nonprofit corporation
6026 Wilshire Boulevard, Los Angeles, California 90036

First published in paperback in 1993 by Sun & Moon Press
10 9 8 7 6 5 4 3 2 1
FIRST EDITION
© Marianne Hauser, 1993
Biographical information © Sun & Moon Press, 1993
All rights reserved

This book was made possible, in part, through a grant from the
Andrew W. Mellon Foundation and through contributions to
The Contemporary Arts Educational Project, Inc.,
a nonprofit corporation
An excerpt from this work was published, in slightly
different form, in *Fiction International*.

Cover: Photograph by Aina Balgalvis
Reprinted by permission of the artist
Design: Katie Messborn

LIBRARY OF CONGRESS CATALOGING IN PUBLICATION DATA
Hauser, Marianne
Me & My Mom
Marianne Hauser. — 1st ed.
p. cm—(Sun & Moon Classics: 36)
ISBN: 1-55713-175-9 : $9.95
1. Mothers and daughters—United States—Fiction.
2. Nursing home patients—United States—Fiction.
I. Title. II. Title: Me and my mom
PS3558.A7587M39 1993
813'.54—dc20 93-26086 CIP

Printed in the United States of America on acid-free paper.

In memory of the unforgettable Coby Gilman

. . . Will you
mother, come quickly,
won't you. Why not

go quietly, be left
with a memory
or an insinuation or two
of cracks in pavement.

Robert Creeley

Tell her a funny story. Make her laugh. But keep the visit to a minimum. Remember, with her brief attention span only the moment counts, from moment to moment. Those moments multiply like mice and the longer I stay the tougher for the two of us when I kiss her goodbye. Any pretext will do to hold me. She is out of cigarettes. Would I buy her a pack? Would I help her get up to the roof? She is dying for a glimpse of the house where she used to live.

But at the Bide-a-Wee Nursing Home smoking is against the rules. And access to the roof was barred after a paraplegic managed to hurl herself across the security rail into the street. Of course mom may have forgotten.

She forgets yet she remembers. That's why her company can become eerie. I hate to stay a full hour. But once I split I'm trapped anew by that godawful guilt as she waves at me from the wheelchair, her face awash with tears but bravely smiling.

ॐ

I'm ambling down the long street to the Bide-a-Wee and her face looms at an improbable distance maybe from a cloud in the autumn sky, maybe from a child's crazy kite in the early spring wind. Her skin is cracked like dried-out potting soil. But her face is larger than life and older than time.

ॐ

What's the time? Shoulda left home later. Am much too early. They'll still be at lunch, with mom seated next to this senile Romeo who promptly nods off between courses. And each time he wakes up he makes a grab for mom. She has demanded a different table. No dice. Seating is arranged by alphabet. That, she was told by the management, is a rule which must not be broken.

The help call him lover boy. He tries to feel up any female within reach. Some get a kick out of it. There's lots of shrieks and giggles. If nothing more, he entertains them in competition with the TV at the far end of the dining hall which converts into the "recreation area" between meals.

Does he still get a hard-on—at his age? I wonder.

Does mom wonder?

ও

One ought to have compassion for one's fellow inmates, mom will say, alluding to her fellow residents. (The management speaks of them as "our guests".) However, their compulsive behavior makes it extremely difficult to sympathize. The mannerisms! The endless repetition of a phrase or a word, predictable like TV gibberish! she may sigh into a Diet Coke commercial. In this place, the nonsensical is the norm.

Mom is surveying the TV-hooked assembly of Bide-a-Weeans like far out exotic folk. Is there a logical pattern to their obsessions? Does it give them pleasure to repeat and repeat? Oh those protracted echoes of the void. . . .

She clutches at her head. She puts on her glasses and ruffles the pages of the book in her lap. I've recognized the book at once, and I jump up to say goodbye. Am awful busy, mom.

I understand. Still, if you could spare a few moments. . . .
I thought I would read you a paragraph from a story by. . . .

She pauses. I squirm while she thumbs through the tattered volume, its pages flecked with age, the binding held together by a thread.

It won't take long. May I? It's only a paragraph. (No not that mile long paragraph again not that old chestnut) Yes mom, you may.

You will appreciate the style. The narration resembles a spiral stairway which only a master like. . . . Damn! I have lost the author's name.

Think of the letter *J*, I suggest, being helpful. Jessie and Frank would be too common for you, I add, being nasty. But she is smiling.

Of course! The name was on the tip of my tongue. In fact it is on the front page. . . .

So it is, mom. Shoot.

I grit my teeth. I plump down in the chair and suffer while she reads me the same mile long paragraph I've heard a trillion times before and still can't see why it's worth repeating even once.

᠀

Half an hour to kill. If I arrive now, I'll be stuck among wheelchairs and walkers struggling for first place in the elevator. Out they come wheeling from the dining hall into the hallway in a reek of cabbage and urine; mumbling, jostling, snarling. Bumping each other. A caravan of gray heads. They maneuver around the bend and past the daily announcement chalked on the blackboard by the reception desk:

> *The Temperature*
> *The Day*
> *The Month*
> *The Year*
> *The Sun sets When*

The last piece of info irritates mom beyond reason. In this place, she says, the sun neither rises nor sets. I have seen no sun in this place.

I tell her that we on the outside have the same problem because of the smog.

I've slipped into my parka, anxious to leave.

I was not speaking of *your* sun, mom says.

৯

It must be weird to be so old. I'd rather pass up the honor. I assure her that the Bide-a-Wee management is doing its best. Maybe I'm overstating my case, but where else can I put her? She can't stay with us. We'd be at each other's throat, me and Jack and the baby in one small apartment. Chances are she thinks I've written her off. I'm only guessing. If there's rage and turmoil in her head she won't let on. These days she rarely complains. Perhaps she has resigned herself. Or is she being cagey? Whatever. The staff says it is an improvement.

৯

Her first days at the Bide-a-Wee were a nightmare. It wiped me out, her acting like a wild animal, clawing and biting and shouting for all to hear that her daughter had stuck her into an insane asylum to be rid of her once and for all. This when I had worn myself to a frazzle, shopping for a decent, affordable nursing home! Some of the places I looked into—I wouldn't be caught dead in any of them. The Bide-a-Wee isn't the Hilton. But it's heaven compared to those dumps.

She was fighting the staff so hard they strapped her to the wheelchair, afraid she might do herself bodily harm, they explained, though I suspect they were more afraid we'd sue in case she did harm herself. She was given injections and fed I still don't know what drugs—vitamins, they said when I asked. I was so stressed out I had to smoke a joint in the toilet to feel sufficiently relaxed to face the doctor.

ॐ

A rather ancient guy with a straggly beard and a sardonic squint in his eyes. Definitely not your AMA type. He is accessible, unlike those arrogant physicians who make you pay before they deign to look at you.

But money was not involved. He said he had retired from private practice. He was the doctor on call at the Bide-a-Wee, overworked and underpaid and despised by the management. He said he came with the house.

Did mom have a drinking problem? he inquired. Sort of, I mumbled. The question embarrassed me. I blushed, and he quickly assured me that alcoholism was a common problem among the aged.

They have to drown their alienation somehow. Science keeps expanding their life span in proportion to the shrinking quality of their lives. Would you care for a cup of coffee?

ॐ

We have coffee and doughnuts at a nearby fast food joint where he elaborates on the barbarism of enforced longevity—a formidable gold mine for geriatricians and research professors in search of the Nobel Prize, but a cruel hoax on the old, especially on the multitudes of the impoverished old.

The doctor snorts. He lights a cigarette and inhales with desperate zeal. The old, the old—they have to be fed. But where's the feedback? They are the hidden cancer which is gnawing at the bowels of our great land! he orates with such sudden, well-faked passion, you'd think he was switching sides. Free enterprise, democracy are doomed unless we remove the cancer. But what surgical procedure should be applied?

The doctor looks up at the greasy ceiling. Allow me to make a modest proposal, he says in a pious tone. Let us recruit the huddled masses of our impoverished old into the armed forces and employ them as shock troops in the next war. Then the enemy will slaughter them for us. It may sound drastic, but it is expedient. Alive, they remain a deadly threat to the economy, and a troubling, ever present memento mori.

Like those growing mountains of garbage we can't decide where to bury, I interrupt. This is a sick world. Thank god he hasn't yet hit me with personal data. I'm too wiped out to sit through a parody on uncaring kids not taking poor old mom into their home etcetera.

But I am not uncaring and I want him to know it. When will they stop strapping her to the chair? I ask. When will they stop feeding her downers? And I emphasize that I picked the Bide-a-Wee for my mom because it has an A+ rating.

It has? Doc signals for the check and grinds his cigarette into the empty cup. Institutions are institutions, whether for lunatics, criminals or old folks. As to harness and tranquilizers, she soon won't need them anymore.

You have to realize, he says as he pays half of the tab, that an institution per se is the most effective tranquilizer known to man.

ऒ

His prognosis is correct. Security belts and downers are history. Now her self control marks such a drastic reversal, it strikes me as a reproach.

I have learned my lesson, she says. Here one learns how to avoid punishment, though hardly humiliation.

She may be alluding to a recent incident during the daily afternoon snack. Two cookies and a dixie cup of apple juice for each were passed around by an aide when mom requested an untouched cup. Her's seemed to have lipstick on it. And it was leaking.

You sure it ain't somethin else that's leakin', young lady? The aide, a husky male, was grinning and feeling under mom's seat.

We are not thirsty anymore. Thank you. Mom's tone was quiet. But her face had turned white.

In former days she would not have tolerated such humiliation. But an institution is a tranquilizer, just like doc explained to me.

ऒ

Here one learns to keep one's mouth shut, mom will say. Here one has lost not only the right to dissent, but the right over one's life and death.

Is she thinking of the paraplegic who threw herself off the roof? The management's reaction to the suicide was expectedly low key. They called it an unfortunate accident and sealed off entrance to the roof. As for the media, they ignored the whole matter. They have bloodier horrors available to improve their ratings.

I'm not sure why I mention the suicide when the subject might upset her. But she keeps her cool. It must have been an incredible feat, she says with a spark of admiration. The poor woman, surely depressed beyond words, braves the barbed wire guard and lets herself roll down six floors into the yard. The mangled body was found by a field worker from the Department for the Aging. Yes, life has its ironies. One assumes she would have preferred a less conspicuous quietus—an overdose of sleeping pills, for instance. But here it is impossible to hide anything, not even a bite of food or a drop of bourbon for a nightcap. The rooms are regularly searched. I needn't add that one's garments aren't safe from inspection either.

She gazes out the window at a sparrow. I so miss my cats, she says.

ও

I shouldn't sit down in the vest-pocket park with the homeless. But where else is a body to sit in this stinking city? Again I'm too early for mom. I dread visiting her. And yet again and again I'm heading her way much too early.

They are scattered about me on benches and in the trampled, yellowed grass, bundles of leftover life under tattered rags or rugs. Wish my old social science prof was here to learn what's doing in his own backyard. He never included those desamparados into his lectures. He always slobbered over the ones south of the border. A real old fashioned liberal. I dropped his course.

ॐ

They are watching me from under their rags. I can't see their eyes. But I feel them crawl over my clothes, sizing me up across bundles of newsprint, bulwarks of outadate uptodate disinformation. The black hole has sucked up calendar logic and mom's memory clock may be running OK when it jumbles time.

ॐ

I have no business sitting here, me in my pre-washed jeans slit and frazzled at the knees for that funky look—a fashion fad mom calls an affront to the poor. She's right. But the jeans were on sale. So I wear them.

No, they aren't staring at my clothes. I've trespassed on their turf, that's why they are staring. I am the enemy.

Fuckem. Shut your eyes behind your shades and spirit them away like so:

> *dear homeless please*
> *go away*
> *quit my vest-pocket*
> *park*
> *any old place*
> *in the subway*
> *under the bridges*
> *GO*

ॐ

Let them stare. Ain't no skin off my ass. I ought to be used to it from the Bide-a-Wee. When I weave my way through the wheelchair and walker battalions, the oldies give me the same dirty look. The elderly. OK I stand corrected. But what a name tag! It puts them under one hat with the homeless for god and country. Umpteen decrepit people scrabbling under one hat. Freaks you out. I'd love to hear mom's view. But she has dreamed herself into a past that perhaps never was, a youth that perhaps never was her life. She'll be sitting in the farthest corner by the window, far away from the rest. Mom keeps to herself.

ᨚ

Flyer from a PR package available free at reception desk:

To neutralize behavioral patterns of an anti-social character, a counter-productive, not infrequently encountered tendency resulting from overly excessive self-absorption, we encourage our seniors to circulate within the limits of their capability, so as to interact with their fellow seniors through meaningful dialogue.

> *The Management of the Bide-a-Wee*
> A modern care facility for the aged
> (Founded in 1901)

ᨚ

I hand mom the flyer for laughs. But she doesn't even crack a smile. She slowly reads through the text, then reads over it again laboriously word for word, lips moving along as her index finger traces the lines.

Mom used to be a proofreader. Is it possible that her mind has regressed to the old nine-to-five job?

(An indication of senility. I am alarmed.)

Mom, once you've finished, you can tear it up.

I may never finish. She makes a face and sighs. Her attempt at translating this sorry specimen of managerial confusion into a semblance of English seems to lead into a deadend street. She can't decipher the meaning behind the verbiage. Obviously we are dealing with the work of a defective brain or computer or both.

(Not all that senile after all, thank god!)

Mom has removed her glasses and is folding the flyer into a precise square. She may preserve it as a document of our time. She may even give it another try during the night. It will be a change from crossword puzzles, and a more potent soporific.

I give her a big hug. I love you, mom.

I love you too. Watch out, child! I'm afraid you are choking me!

☙

My poor sweet dreadful old mom. She stays aloof. She stays in the farthest corner in self-imposed exile, her wheelchair turned to face the window. The other residents have stopped approaching her. Let her be. She fancies herself above us, that hoity-toity phony upper crust old dame who eats with her fork inside out like foreigners do, but this is America.

Mom is satisfied that they leave her alone although she regrets their appraisal. Here class distinctions don't exist, she says. We are all in the same hole, equally degraded and ignored. Perhaps my upbringing sets me apart from, but hardly above the others. Why must I socialize, to employ that ridiculous term? I have nothing to say that anyone would care to hear. The feeling, I assume, is reciprocal.

ફ

She scans the dining hall, the inmates chatting against the ongoing noise of the TV. They talk and talk to convince themselves that they are alive, mom supposes. Most often they talk for their own ears, although a few no longer can talk. They have sunk into irretrievable silence as happened to your great-grandfather on the west deck of our summer cottage. The sunset over the lake and the distant hills was of such astounding beauty. . . .

She moistens her lips. Sit down. I will tell you his tale.

I reluctantly pull out a chair. She's told me about him so often, his ghost might sneak into my dreams, into bed with me as my lover. He comes in all sorts of disguises. In one dream he was wearing mom's elegant big white hat.

Your great-grandfather. . . .

Yes, mom. I lean back and cross my arms, resigned.

He was a brilliant defense attorney and a dedicated member of the senate. Tall, and outrageously handsome. Wait . . . I may have his photo somewhere. . . .

She stares into space. The sepia has faded. . . . I'm afraid the face on the picture was badly damaged. . . .

A long pause. Who else will crawl out of mom's memory closet? Not my dad. She almost never mentions him. I was three when he left through the back door. He never returned. For me he is not even a memory, only a flickering image in an antique never-to-be-restored silent film.

What are you thinking of, my child?
Nothing, mom.

ॐ

Your great grandfather. . . . He was not yet seventy when
he lost his speech, no one could understand why. He appeared in robust health. . . . Athletic. . . . Cockswain at Har-
vard. . . . At dusk he took me on long walks around the
lake. . . . Winters I would slip under his long raccoon coat.
He held me tight to keep me warm. I loved him so. . . .

She is stroking the worn suede of her purse.

The senator as pedophile? My mind takes an unsched-
uled side trip. Mom was a very pretty little girl. She's shown
me pictures. Lolita in a brief, flounced frock. What if. . . .

She has emptied the purse into her lap. A fragrant sliver
of soap. A bunch of keys. An uncancelled one-way ticket to
Rockland, Maine. A gold locket with the blurred mini-mini-
ature of a baby.

A small easter egg wrapped in worn pink foil has rolled
off her lap and into dusty oblivion.

I can't imagine where I left my cigarettes. . . .

She is talking to herself. I blow her a kiss and escape.

ॐ

Her eyelids are red and swollen and her hair is drooping
down her face in messy strands. She needs a trim. But so far
she hasn't allowed me close, not with my scissors.

Don't touch my hair!

She shrinks in the chair and shields her breasts like I was
about to attack her.

My hair does not concern you. Put those scissors away
and leave me alone. Now!

I leave. What else can I do. She has been acting hostile or suspicious ever since Claudio stopped coming to the Bide-a-Wee to do her hair.

ﶠ

Claudio, her favorite hairdresser. She'd come to his shop when she could still get about. Even when she had to use the walker, she managed. Later, he made it his mission to come to her.

He'd show at the Bide-a-Wee Sunday mornings. The Lord would absolve him if he absented himself from mass to maintain the coiffure of his dearest client. That's how he talked. And she loved it.

A neat looking guy. Not exactly my type, but hers, you may be sure. Mom is partial to old world charm and he had plenty, what with his elegant manners and silk scarves and the pretty face of a dissipated altar boy, not to mention his Spanish accent which rolled around his tongue like foreplay. And he was less than half her age.

Mom always has fallen for younger men. I was in junior high when this young guy steps out of the bathroom stark naked. That was in the middle of the night and I had to go to the john. We bumped into each other, me on my way in, he on his way out. He said he was sorry and covered himself with a towel.

Next morning while we get ready, me for school and mom for work, I ask her about the guy. The guy? Oh yes, he is just a friend. We're friends, that's all, she says and puts her big hat on in front of the hall mirror.

Oh yeah? I say into the mirror. And I see my wide grin under the wide, floppy brim of her hat.

Oh, yeah? I call from the bedroom and steal her Shalimar.

Was his complexion dark, like Claudio's? And did he have a Spanish accent as well? I could almost swear that he did.

❧

Claudio's accent, that seductive beat—it must have drawn her into fantasies of past courtships or loves and his visits were more vital to her than mine or anyone else's, though few visitors came, friends had moved away or were too busy or decrepit. And most were dead.

But anyway, at that point only Claudio counted. She'd receive him in the hallway, dressed in her black silk kimono with the Japanese symbol for happiness stamped in gold. He'd kiss her hand and wheel her into the elevator and to her room 49, which is a cubicle with half a window and a wash basin and a plastic chair and a bed.

We have arrived, he sang. Now I will give the señora the works.

And so he did: shampoo, a silver rinse, a smart trim and a blow-dry, all free of charge. For she was, he intoned, his senora encantadora, and she had tipped him well in the old days.

❧

I watched them one morning. His long bronze fingers were playing trills and runs in her hair as she sat with her eyes closed and her neck curved toward the ceiling—rapt as I'd seen her only once before, at a concert, during a performance of the *Appassionata*.

When your beautiful mama leaves the asilo, I will fly her to my country and present her to my family. They live in a little village not far from Sevilla. She will be among good people, olive trees, guitars and roses. Please hand me the dryer.

≥&

That was the last we saw of him. He simply disappeared— dying of AIDS, I learned. I could barely bring myself to break the news to mom.

But she refused to believe me. She had heard of AIDS. But she must have forgotten. Why would a healthy young man be suddenly dying? It made no sense. Don't play games with me, she said. He has betrayed my trust in him, I know. I was a fool.

I couldn't get through to her, no matter how often I repeated that he was in the hospital, near death, mom, for chrissake mom DYING! Maybe already dead.

She would not accept it. Claudio had let her down, had slammed the door on her without a goodbye. She would have bet her life on his integrity. But he had none. He turned out to be another coward.

She wouldn't elaborate further. But I'm positive she was referring to dad and I felt sorry for her. But I also felt impatient, and disgusted. An old woman carrying on like a teenager—it was too much. It was sick.

I haven't stopped feeling sorry for her. But her sentiments turn me off, though deep down I know I'm dead wrong. She's been left with a broken heart as they say, whoever they are, whatever they mean by it, I call it a broken dream. I've had plenty of them. But so far I've been able to pick up the pieces and start a new dream, whereas mom. . . .

≥&

Drop it. Claudio died months ago and she no longer mentions his name. She may have forgotten him.

Out of sight out of mind. But not for me. In my mind he is alive in Sevilla, serenading me with his guitar from across a silvery grove of olive trees and scarlet roses.

ه

> *i love claudio*
> *claudio loves me*

carved with a Swiss army knife into my desk top at junior high.

Did mom love Claudio? I mean did she want to sleep with him? At her age?

In my view sex equals youth or vice versa period, though when I was in my early teens I called my ex-boyfriend a pervert for dating a dame of twenty. Live and learn.

Does mom have sex dreams? I raise the issue with my husband after we've done the dishes.

None of your bee's wax, honey. Do we have another six-pack in the fridge?

Jack has his own method of setting me straight. When I get off the deep end, he gets down to basics and mom likes him fine though she must be conscious of the vast gap between them regarding "class." She is too civilized to bring it up, although she has corrected his grammar.

Class! I ask you: what class? Old money type WASP minus the bread? Get real, mom. Jack's my man. These days, with AIDS and everything else fucked up like the ozone layer, we'd better not be classy, and enjoy what we can get.

ه

Biding my time before Bide-a-Wee time. The wind is blowing through the vest-pocket park and a stray cat is slinking around the trash bin. A ravaged tabby, not sleek like mom's tabby, her favorite among four cats. Four spoiled felines were too much for me to deal with after the hard time she gave me when I moved her to the Bide-a-Wee. So I dropped them at the SPCA, never dreaming that the cats would be put to sleep.

(Didn't have the guts to tell her. Pretended I farmed them out with "a nice family.")

She may have forgotten Claudio. But she still asks about the cats.

ba.

Here, puss. . . .

But the stray is busy with the garbage. Dry leaves are falling on empty benches and the park looks bleaker than ever, now that the cops have chased the homeless out.

They ordered them to "vacate the area." The lingo was cop routine. But they weren't acting rough. Maybe the brass had given instructions to keep a low profile. Some videotapes must have given the men a bad image and the PD needed a facelift.

Gotta watch your step or what you step into, and that goes for all of us. What with home video such a popular toy from bedroom to park bench, the camera has an eye on you, just like god.

ba.

The cops got the job done without any hassle. The homeless peeled themselves out of their rags, coughing and squinting; confused like Bide-a-Wee inmates in a sudden rush of light. Some grumbled. But no one protested, not even the bearded guy who looked like a black version of Abbie Hoffman on TV before he was offed.

Perhaps I should be protesting. But I hate to get involved. Besides, I'm already on a different trip, back into the past, like mom. I'm in my first year at junior high, on my way home from school when I'm stopped by a big parade. Dark flags. Dark drums and shouting.

> *hey hey*
> *LBJ*
> *how many kids*
> *did you kill today*

I've slipped through the police barrier for a better view. A black coffin, huge enough to fill a class of kids my size, is marching past. The pallbearers are hooded in black and their faces are spooky white death masks.

Hey, hey. . . . the masks are shouting at me. I'm scared to death and off I race, with the rumble of drums at my back like approaching thunder.

That was a thousand years ago. But when I think of it I get scared like it was today.

❧

Left-behind newspapers take off from vacant benches and land in the trees. The park's been cleaned up all right. Skinheads and noheads in nail-studded leather are marching past and out of sight. Behind the tall spike fence a boom-box-eardrum-blaster blares forth hard metal, soft news;

space-stationed instant uncensored misinformation transmitted live by the dead.

Should I join a peace group? Make war on war?

> *get wise kid*
> *it's only a conflict*
> *computerized by the lord*
> *slam bang crash and*
> WOW
> *how many kids?*
> *no body counts*
> *this time around*
> *sorry kiddo*

ঌ

On a recent visit to the Bide-a-Wee, a scrap of paper fell from mom's blouse. She didn't notice and I picked it up. The page was jagged like she had torn it off a yellow scratchpad in a hurry. And the writing on it was shaky—quite different from her former determined hand.

I read through it. She didn't seem to notice.

Another casualty at the asylum. Today, at table, my dinner companion, the gentleman nicknamed Romeo or Casanova, dropped dead. His departure, sudden but by no means unexpected, seemed to rejuvenate many of our inmates. The dining hall was abuzz with vitality. There was chatter and even laughter. I shall not dwell on my own reaction.

Does mom keep a diary? I wonder why the possibility has me worried.

ঌ

When you checked me in, she says, you did not merely sign over my social security and retirement pay to them. You signed over my life.

I defend myself for the hundredth time. Step by step I spell out the financial arrangement on which the Bide-a-Wee insists before admission. Everybody has to sign the same agreement. It's one of their rules.

I am not everybody. Nobody is, she says. Conformity breeds evil. Permit them to control your income, and they control your life body and soul.

She adds something about my having signed away her dignity. But I don't pay attention. My hate is all at once so fierce I could kill her for dumping on me and putting me on the defense. I'm guilty of nothing. What am I supposed to do—check her out and take her in so we'll be at each other's throat? Our apartment is already so cramped, you can't breathe. And who's there to look after her? Not the neighbors who look after the baby while I'm away, slaving as a DEO which is about the lowest you can get as a computer operator. Punching keys, we used to call it. And half the time Jack's either out of a job or out, job hunting. But has she ever asked me how we manage?

I'm beside myself with indignation. Stop blaming me, mother!

Blame you? Why would I blame you? For what?

Skip it! I yank the wheelchair to the side and her head snaps back like a doll's.

O dear . . . She claps a hand to her mouth. O dear, I'm so terribly sorry. . . . I just lost control over my bladder. . . .

❧

Poor mom. She tries to hold it in—her rage, her shame. Her desperation and her urine. There is no exit from her hell. She knows it and she does not know it. She makes plans for a long weekend with friends in the country, friends she hasn't seen in twenty years. Their phone number and they themselves are most likely extinct. But she quickly forgets what she planned. At least she won't feel cheated when her projects don't pan out. Sometimes her quirky memory can be a blessing.

➠

She makes plans to move back into her old apartment which she remembers as it used to be, uncluttered, cheerful, elegant and airy and not the stinking mess from which I saved her. Yes. My moving her into the Bide-a-Wee saved her from worse. I really must stop feeling guilty.

She couldn't have survived for long, living alone, hobbling about on her walker through food scraps and kitty litter. The dirty laundry was piling up and half empty bottles were rolling out from under the unmade bed. The spilled booze was enough to turn her cats into alcoholics. The place was a nightmare.

At that point she was really hitting the bottle. She wasn't a nasty drunk. But she rarely was sober—at constant risk of falling and breaking her bones. And mom was especially accident-prone since her legs had become paralyzed thanks to a sleazebag doctor who sweet-talked her into surgery to relieve back pain from a slipped disk.

The pain is gone. So are her legs. But not once has she spoken against the doctor. While me, I always stand accused of every single one of her misfortunes.

⋅⋅

Jack says I shoulda let her stay at home and drink herself to heaven rather than have her vegetate with a bunch of tottering loonies. But she isn't his mom, and he is hardly the one to hand out advice when he lost two jobs in a row, showing up for work drunk.

⋅⋅

Mom wasn't smashed. But she wasn't sober when I broached the Bide-a-Wee topic as gently as was feasible, considering. It wouldn't be easy. She loved her home and wasn't likely to surrender it without a fight. But I was unprepared for her crazed resistance. Not in my wildest dreams had I imagined what anger was seething beneath the surface.

The insults she spat at me! Shameless conniver . . . despicable coward. . . . Those were the milder invectives. She raged that I had schemed behind her back, that I would lock her up in an asylum so I'd be free to get my hands on what little she possessed. Surely, my devious brain should have construed a less vicious, less obvious method to dispose of her, she raged.

Supposing you want to get rid of a cat, would you drop the helpless creature at the SPCA? Answer me!

(That one still makes me wince today. But at the time, while her cats were playing tag with the rotting garbage, it was just another preposterous metaphor.)

I refuse to honor your ultimatum. You'll have to kill me before you drag me away. This is my house. Get out and plot some different method to get rid of your mother!

Mom! Nobody wants to get rid of you. . . .

Out of my house! Out! I shall call the police.

I snatched the phone from her and begged her to let me explain. But she had heaved herself into the corridor and was yelling for help. Doors were opening when I succeeded in pulling her back into the apartment.

Be reasonable, mom. We only want what's best for you.

Liar! You want what is best for yourself!

She tripped me with the walker. I screamed and landed on my back in the cat shit.

Now, as I reflect on the scene, it looks like a black comedy. But when it happened, it was unqualified horror. I hadn't hurt myself. But in all my life I had never felt quite so abandoned. And I bawled like a baby.

ॐ

I didn't mean to hurt you. . . . My poor baby. . . .

She made an effort to bend down and help me up, it was pathetic, I said OK I'm OK honest I am mom and I pulled myself back on my feet with the walker and when I saw her cry I stuck my head between her breasts and cried all over again.

So there we were, both of us holding on to that orthopedic contraption and crying together like there was no tomorrow.

ॐ

Each time I take off for the Bide-a-Wee I wish by god I had some company. Anyone's, even a stranger's would help ease the tension. At first a friend or acquaintance would volunteer. Now everyone has an excuse. I'd probably act the same if I were in their shoes. Old people tend to get on one's nerves. But that isn't the worst of it. Simply staying in their presence for a while can turn spooky—like holding vigil at your own wake.

Increasingly, as I sit with her, I have the creepy sensation that I am caught in a time warp, that she is a future me.

Last night in a dream I was in her wheelchair, alive but dead. A classic sci-fi situation, but so real, I woke up with a scream and the scream woke the baby and the baby screamed and woke Jack.

੩

Perhaps the eager Rev. Somethingorother wouldn't mind sitting with mom. But she can't stand the sight of him. When he appeared at the Bide-a-Wee on his *Pray-athon through the Homes of Mature Seniors* she hurriedly whisked herself out of the dining hall.

She had met him on TV although she rarely watches. But that time she was duped by a program change. Instead of Rubinstein at the piano, the preach popped up from behind an enormous neon cross in a garden of pretty maidens draped in the Stripes and the Stars. The staging and his call for instant happiness via a prayer hook-up with the almighty so grossed her out, she pressed the off button to the catcalls of devoted viewers.

੩

God knows why he is so anxious to meet with mom. Maybe because of her upper-class manners someone marked her out as well-connected. I've heard rumors to that effect. But if she had connections, why the hell would she live at the Bide-a-Wee? Jack and me we can't even wheedle a small loan out of the bank. The family loot went down the drain in the great depression. There is no bread.

But rumors are born on the wings of prayer, as mom used to say. The preach is a man of faith; and in his little black book he may have listed her as a lady down on her luck though with a name still prestigious enough to con some big corporation into helping him finance his new mammoth taj mahal trump type temple for born-again Christers.

ॐ

"Praise god from whom all blessings flow. . . ." The loudspeakers have channeled the offertory into every corner of the building. The service is over and the good reverend, stepping briskly, heads for the hallway and mom.

She tries to flee to the elevator. Too late. He has seized the handgrip of her chair. Greetings! His voice and looks are packed with genial fellowship. No dreary cleric clothes for him. He sports light tweeds and a Rotary pin. Greetings! he beams, brandishing a glossy paperback, pristine in its plastic wrappings: the latest updated version of the revised gospel and a free gift for the ladies!

A free gift? Free of what? mom demands cold as ice. When her ear for language is offended she can cut you down to size. I ought to know.

The sudden put-down can annoy the bejeezus out of you though I realize it's in her blood. Her genes must be buzzing with wasps. But today, as they buzz to the surface, it's fun watching them sting. It's fun, her telling him in clipped syllables that she does not intend to trade her old family bible for a new model. She has heard enough, having heard him market Christianity like a moisturizer. The loudspeaker system carried his sermon into the hallway. She was his captive audience.

Now he is her captive audience. But is he listening? Hands folded over the rejected free gift bible he waits her out while she tells him off, exhorting him for his "paean to youth" at the expense of the old—at an old people's home, of all places! His sheep may not perceive the insult. However, she is not his sheep.

Amen, he murmurs. But is he listening?

Pray as you pay and—hallelujah—wrinkles and crows-feet have vanished. Is that how you construe god's word? she demands, though religion is the last thing on her mind. True, she was raised an Anglican—a faith where god can be trusted to be a gentleman, she might remark. But she isn't a church goer.

No, what enrages her about the preach is his implied denunciation of aging as something loathsome, a horrid infliction to be denied, a cardinal sin which only his brand of holiness can wash away.

You are promoting a cosmetic universe, created not by god but by television. When I try to visualize your heaven, I can only shudder.

Mom actually shudders and buttons her jacket up to the neck. I am an old woman, she says, weary all at once and quite hoarse. I dream of other melodies. Please go.

ও

She broke into a hacking cough and at last the preach had the floor.

It was a treat to chat with both of you. Now I must run. His tone was hearty, a native twang melting into her cough.

What a heavenly gift to find your mom so trim, he beamed, patting me on the back, slap slap, with a gloved hand. Doesn't show her age, does she now. Looks like a million dollars. I wish I had the time for the three of us to pray together. But I have two other senior centers on my schedule. God bless!

Out he winged into the slushy snow. Never got the message. Never listened. Dysfunctional attention span, just like the oldies. Just like me and anyone else today, kids, grownies, oldies. Same difference.

❧

Eggs Benedict, mom will say out of the clouds. At the Majestic Grand they serve the most delectable Eggs Benedict. He ordered them for Sunday brunch. . . . What was his name?

She is sucking her little finger. Names are evasive. His face eludes me too. But I can see the breakfast room of the hotel, the wide arched windows and on every table a single rose. . . .

One long-stemmed dark red rose freshly cut. You can always tell by the fragrance. And the Eggs Benedict was perfectly seasoned. . . . He was an architect, I now recall. But his name. . . .

She sniffs the air and shades her eyes. I waited for him in the lobby. He came down in the lift—a gilded open cage elevator equipped with the tapestried bench of another age when the Majesticplayed host to the crème de la crème—Edwardian royalty, busty prima donnas, international financiers and our own robber barons, naturally. Of course that was before my time, I think. . . .

Mom and the architect: were they lovers?

She does not react. She is moving her arm in a curve to indicate the lobby ceiling, a high domed whimsy of cupids, pastel clouds and nudes à la Fragonard.

Fragonard. Is that the architect's name?

But she does not respond. She is too deep into her past, alone (with him?) in the morning light in the grand ballroom. Mirror walls reflect infinities of chandeliers. Rainbow prisms self-reflect and tinkle.

We did the foxtrot on the mirror slick parquet to the childhood tinkle of my old music box. . . .

I gasp. Who is making this up—me or my mom?

In retrospect, she says, it does seem odd, it is. But their Eggs Benedict is out of this world. One Sunday when we go for brunch together you must taste it.

ॐ

By now she has taken me on so many trips, I am an exhausted tourist. Sometimes she'd guide me exclusively through the interior of the Majestic Grand. At others she would walk me up and down in front of the building and urge me to concentrate on the rich facade, the Gothic gargoyles, Grecian columns; the Renaissance friezes and Romanesque turrets, all fused into one symphony of stone.

I might be auditing a cram course in American mid-nineteenth century architecture. And I'd interrupt to ask if the architect was her tutor.

I may never find out. Always the excursion would end in the breakfast room, at the table by the window in the sun, with the Eggs Benedict the ultimate center piece.

ॐ

Me and mom at the Majestic for brunch: it is one of her many pipedreams, quickly forgotten, reborn and forgotten again. But not today. Today she is determined to realize the dream.

I've barely arrived out of a heavy downpour when she confronts me with her strategy. No reason why we can't leave for the Majestic as soon as next Sunday, she whispers. Move closer. Here is my plan.

Hold it! I've shouted and she cautions me to lower my voice. The Bide-a-Wee mustn't get wind of our conspiracy. You can't tell where they plant their spies. Now listen carefully.

She is in high spirits—an aged child scheming to pull a fast one on teacher. Last night, when she couldn't sleep, she devised a plan so simple it made her laugh. She'd ask the doctor to obtain a pass for her to go outside for X-rays or some other emergency. I'd have a taxi ready and we'd be off for the Majestic Grand.

Hold it, mom! I'm leaning over her, my hair dripping with rain.

Mom says she hopes it won't be raining next Sunday. Without sunshine, the breakfast room at the Majestic. . . .

Forget the Majestic! I cry in a frenzy and she looks at me in utter astonishment. Forget the Majestic? Forget the last surviving monument to grandeur in a city of highrise monotony and low taste? Forget the cornices and gilded turrets? The leafy capitals ringed by arcane flowers? Mom wipes the damp window and scans the fog for the stone flowers in the rain.

I relax. The danger has passed. Another moment and she will be far away in space like she's spaced out. She would think I was making it up if I told her the truth: that the Majestic deteriorated and became a flea bag hotel years ago, until it collapsed overnight—as recently as last week, I seem to remember.

૨&

I've been downtown to stare at the devastation. Chunks of broken masonry and splintered beams. Rusted girders. Mattress springs. Pipes bent into eerie shapes. A forsaken battle zone with the maimed and dead cleared away.

Shadow people poke in clouds of dust. And high above in the blue, suspended from a stretch of wiring, a rectangular shaving mirror. It twists and throws back the sun in a blinding flash—an irrational random survivor.

Few people survived. They return to sift through the rubble. If any remains of mom's grand dream were spared, they were salvaged by savvy collectors. What's left is junk.

I spot a beat-up shoe, a busted toilet. I shield my eyes against the sun and recognize the squashed trumpet of an old gramophone. Nothing of value. Still, people load the stuff into bags and carts. They may be the surviving SROs or homeless. Jack tells me the city housed them by the dozen at the Majestic, fully aware that the hotel had violated every single safety regulation in the book and shoulda been declared off limits except for the rats.

૨&

Corruption from top to bottom and vice versa. Jack got me wise as to how our city is run. He was a clerk for the Housing Preservation Department, or HPD, though hearing him talk HDD, or Housing Destruction Department, seems more to the point. He had a lot of dirt on them. He bothered the wrong people with the wrong questions, and so they terminated him. That was before the Majestic collapsed. He blames the city for the death of I forget how many hundreds.

Not that the HPD hadn't been warned! He says they were swamped with phone calls and letters about cracked walls and shaky floors and flooded community showers and toilets shooting the shit through missing tiles down to the floors below. The complaints came mainly from elderly steadies who had no voice and no other place to go; Bide-a-Wee types, scared for their lives because of drug deals in the elevators and shoot-outs in the corridors and the whole fuckin' dump ready to cave in on them.

The last chandelier that hadn't yet been vandalized or stolen, crashed from the lobby ceiling onto a druggie who was lying spread-eagle on mom's desecrated marble floor. It coulda killed him. But he had already ODed.

ಶಿ

You oughta tell your mom, says Jack. She has a right to know about the real world. Tell her. One day she'll thank you for it.

And what day would that be? For crying out loud, use your head!

Jack is a sweetheart. But sometimes he's just plain dumb.

ಶಿ

Each time mom dragged me on another sightseeing tour through the Majestic, I felt like screaming. But now that I've watched its sorry remains carted off in bits and pieces, I can connect with her dream. Even the Eggs Benedict she's apt to mention apropos of nothing make my mouth water.

She pictures them with the precision of an obsessed chef: poached farm fresh eggs on a split muffin toasted to the right crispness. On top of it a paper-thin lean rosy strip of ham and ah—the heady flavor of the sauce hollandaise. . . . In her mouth, the dish becomes a celebration of love. But the architect—what about him?

I keep asking her and she keeps forgetting how or why or where or who he was.

※

No clues from mom. So I invent him for myself. The dark strong silent type. Pole vault champion. Long distance runner. Perfect vertically and horizontally. Chess master and master at foreplay. We tear each other's clothes off and roll on the floor of his plush suite at mom's Majestic Grand. Wild kissing. Wilder orgasms. The best fuck ever on his thick carpet while me and Jack are having our twice-a-week go on the convertible sofa.

You sure love my doing it to you, don't ya, hon, says Jack and he pats my ass.

※

Somewhere another war was fought and won. That was last month. But the Bide-a-Wee continues to be giftwrapped in victory bunting. At lunch a yellow ribbon was fished from the succotash, causing a minor commotion of cheers and boos.

Now the tables are cleared for afternoon bingo. Most residents are completing their nap upstairs, while a few have stayed in the dining hall to fall asleep in front of a slasher on the TV below *Whistler's Mother*. All is calm.

But wait, there's mom, hectically wheeling amid the tables in flight from another wheelchair; chased by an ancient pucker-mouthed baldie who entreats her in fluty tones: Stop for me! Please, Lady!

He has maneuvered his chair with astounding deftness and succeeds in blocking her exit. Excuse me, lady! Madam! Excuse me, please!

Excuse you? She glares at him. I find your bizarre behavior extremely offensive!

No offense intended, he assures her in his high, thin voice. His great-grandchildren will be here in the afternoon to drive him home, back to the old family farm in Ohio. She has always struck him as a special lady and he reckons she deserves to hear him perform before he checks out.

And here he carefully raises his posterior off the chair, bends forward and slowly lets go of a prolonged fart.

Now, Bide-a-Weeans fart whenever needed for quick relief. But this is no ordinary fart. It is a skilled performance of musical phrasing: a drawn out wail of the blues as from a lone horn after the ball is over and the lights are dimmed.

Mom's indignation has vanished. She is listening intently, afloat on some heavenly enchantment as though Claudio had returned to do her hair.

The final arpeggio has wafted off into space and she is rubbing her eyes, transfixed.

Truly . . . she breathes. Amazing. . . .

And no odor, madam. Did you notice? It's the puny ones that smell bad.

Amazing . . . mom repeats. The sound swept her back to grandfather's summer cottage, the deck at sundown when

Jamie played the trombone. Her brother Jamie . . . His trombone always made her cry. Of course she was young at the time and most sentimental.

When I was young, he says through puckered lips, my stomach muscles were so hard, you coulda used me for a punching bag. When I was young I played so well through my second mouth, you woulda bet I was The Duke or Charlie Parker.

Mom says that Jamie played the trombone in the army. He fell in the first war, she adds, puzzled as though she did not quite believe that he was dead. They say he died in combat. . . .

Me too, he says proudly, I served in the Great War.

But her interest is fading. Her eyes are glazing over as he dives into a lengthy tale about his army days and his buddies, how they egged him on to perform for laughs. Ignorant doughboys, he grumbles. Too dumb to get it under their thick skulls that this was serious art, doing what he just did for madam today at the Bide-a-Wee or nearly a hundred years ago for the boys in the trenches.

Indeed, mom says vaguely, nodding.

Will over muscle! That is what's at the bottom of my art, he says, shifting his weight. My kind of music is a lifelong hobby. (By profession I was a mailman.) I never did it for money, though I go about it like a pro. Can you follow me, madam?

Mom makes an indistinct sound.

Well then, before I break wind like you heard me, madam, I so completely concentrate on my lower muscles, you'd swear I was in training for the Olympics.

And while mom struggles in vain to stay awake, he illustrates how it is done if you have the gift. Inhale real deep to charge the abdomen I call my bellows. Exhale real slow via the rectum I call my pipe and—presto!—the music blows from my second mouth. You name whatever instrument you like to hear, brass, woodwinds . . . Am I going too fast for you?

Mom wakes up and stares at him.

In gay Paree they know their art, he pipes through crinkled lips. In gay Paree before the Great War, a talent like mine would have packed the music halls and made me a rich man. I coulda been the first American wind breaker.

A windbreaker? But that is a parka, says mom. Is it not?

❧

My left sneaker gets stuck in a pot-hole and I stumble over a character who is lying under a trashed quilt, strung out or dead. I don't lift the quilt to look. A potential druggie or corpse in the street is one mini-frame of a video scene reeling past on my trip to mom's.

Seems life is turning fast into a nonstop TV show or vice versa. It saves me from getting involved. But it keeps me confused. What's real? What's hype? The pot-holes are no hype. The city is falling apart, and Jack, fugitive from the heartland, is beginning to feel homesick for the Midwest—a great place for kids to grow up in, he says.

It sure beats the city. Maybe the time has come to make a move, honey? The countryside is wholesome and green, with plenty of wide open spaces to be your own man.

Perhaps. But I am a woman and I reserve judgment.

❧

I sit down on a crumbling stoop. Clearly, this isn't my day. At the supermarket this morning, while waiting in line for the new cashier to dig the workings of the computerized cash register, I gleaned such gruesome items from the scandal sheets, I nearly threw up.

Of course it's close to my period. I'm prone to mood swings. But today I am so fighting mad at the world including me, I can barely contain myself.

Gotta keep myself in check. Am on my way to mom's—always too early and via the same old detours. Outside the Dairy Queen a manhole has blown its lid. And in my little vest-pocket park the benches have been taken out to spite the homeless and leave me no place to sit. None of which is likely to lift my spirits.

Watch your step! I warn myself as I pass through the security gate of the Bide-a-Wee. Be good to your mom, I warn, even as I tear through the dining hall and burst in on her solitude to start a fight.

Would she kindly explain why she has always rejected me? Always! Throughout my entire life!

An impromptu curtain raiser. She glances up from her book, perplexed. What happened, my child?

Ignored! Shut out! Rejected! That's what happened to your child. You made her into a non-person—why? Why did you do this to me!

Do what? Fingers, lips begin to quiver. What are you saying?

A non-person. You heard me, mother. When my baby brother died I stopped to exist for you. Not a day went by that you didn't carry on about him—the poor little angel! And me?

I was nothing. I was a DOA and I'll be glad to spell it out for you. Dead on Arrival!

She is leaning forward, straining to catch what I am driving at. She doesn't seem to understand. I don't understand myself.

Wake up, mother! We are talking about *that baby*!

Why am I pressing on? It makes no sense. She didn't provoke me. Unless her mere existence has become a provocation.

That baby, mother. Don't pretend you are deaf. For you there's only one child that ever counted and believe me it wasn't me.

You needn't shout. I can hear you. She has reached for my hand. Calm yourself. Is your baby ill?

I shiver and pull away. My baby is fine. It's yours I had to hear about till I was blue in the face. Your one and only baby boy—holy bejeezus, he wasn't a baby, he was a premature thing, deformed, not fit to live and you knew it. But did you face reality? O no, not you, you wallowed in grief, sobbing, agonizing: why did he have to die? It was too much, me just a little kid, I coulda died myself, you laying your pain on me, forcing me to share grown-up sorrows. Maybe something inside me did die. Don't you realize what a tragedy it would have been if he had survived—the puny cripple?

Cripple. Or did I say creep? I don't know what I'm saying. It's too heavy, that crazy reversal of roles—my baby, her baby. I see my face in the windowpane and suddenly I loathe myself so thoroughly, I'd gladly smash the window to smithereens.

ૐ

Shoulda thrashed out my grievances in my teens when I had real problems. Shoulda charged her with misplaced maternal loyalty or love when my life was one mess, she always at work and me into speed and booze and sex at fourteen, sleeping around with all sorts of freaks until I freaked and swallowed her seconal to get out of the mess for good. Only I blew it. As soon as I'd washed down the pills with her Grand Marnier, I blew them back into the toilet.

ૐ

I was lying on her bed in a twilight daze, half asleep half awake as the snow piled up on the windowpane and her oval mirror dissolved in the shadows. Mom was under the patchquilt with me, her voice a long soft lullaby

> *good night my baby*
> *all is well*
> *good night I love you*
>
> *only you*
>
> *I love you best*
>
> *sleep now*
>
> *now you must sleep*
> *sleep tight*
>
> *good night*

and all the while she was holding me in her warmth as I lay rigid like a corpse so she would stay worried for me.

She rocked me, she talked me to sleep. I slept through the night. When I woke up, the snow was a sparkly cushion on the window ledge in the sun and I felt great. But I played sick to keep her worried for me which worked like magic. She didn't leave for the office and I was excused from school.

The whole day was a story book day, she fussing over me, spoon-feeding me my favorite cereal, wiping my mouth, and letting me blow my nose into her lacy sweet-smelling hanky. She drew me a bath and I stayed forever in her pine scented bubbles. And she let me wear her Japanese kimono for luck. It was unadulterated heaven.

Together we were looking out the window at the snow, mom with her arm around me and both of us silent until she asked softly would I care to tell her why I did it?

Not surprisingly she had found the empty seconal container the moment she was back from work. I had dropped it in front of the toilet where she couldn't miss it. Then she would start mourning me because I was dead.

But here I was, happy to be alive, and uncertain where to begin or what to tell or whether to tell anything at all.

Dunno, I finally said. It's something that's been going around in school, like the flu. I guess we're just a bunch of spoiled, lazy, hopeless kids.

Which is exactly what our teacher told us last week after one of our classmates had shot himself through the mouth with his daddy's gun.

⁂

We never did talk it out, the chaos I went through in my teens. So why harp on an even more distant past? It has been ages since she lost her son. I wasn't yet four when he died and she had only me to share her misery. Dad had walked out on her while she was pregnant. Perhaps her grief ran so deep and lasted so long because she had lost two sons? Dad could have been her son, he was way younger than she, a sure winner in looks but no breadwinner. She had to work for a living while he wrote—poetry, I think I heard her say, though I could be one hundred percent wrong. I know that little about my dad or their marriage. Mom has always been a very private lady.

&

I won't ask and she won't talk. So who's to blame? I've learned to deal with my problems no worse than the next guy. She is my one big problem left and I'll have to live with it like forever. So why attack her for what's dead and buried?

But she has already cut off my senseless diatribe with equally senseless advice. Perhaps, she ventures, slowly working her hands as in a waterless cleansing rite, perhaps you would have less problems with your baby if you had breastfed him for another month. . . .

&

All around town they are demolishing buildings and building new ones at such a pace, you'd swear we'd have a brand new city by tomorrow. Not so. Pavements, watermains, subways, tunnels and bridges remain in a lethal state of convulsion.

Mom's apartment house is to come down to make room for an overpriced highrise. Eventually she will have to be told. So far I haven't had the heart.

Since I "evicted" her—mom's term!—I have avoided the place. Too many bad associations. Too many bad vibes. But somebody has to take care of essentials, sort out whatever we can use for ourselves, and leave the remains to the wreckers.

Jack will be taking over for me. His job should be easy. He won't have to work through a clutter of accumulated possessions. Mom's home, unlike her head, is free of the past.

No heavy, solemn heirlooms or fragile minutiae. No family photos, gimcracks or doilies. Except for her ancient books with their brittle pages and cracking spines, she has stayed clear of tangible memories.

Even her grandpa or rather his life-size portrait she donated long ago to a local museum upstate. There is no sign that a very old woman lived here and tried to survive.

ა

Breathless whispers in the dining hall and corridors. Giggles and shocked outcries as ears are bent to catch the latest scandal. Miss Nobody? My stars! She was such a meek little thing. . . .

She was. That's why the nickname stuck to the pint-sized nonagenarian. Her death has brought the Bide-a-Wee to life—a not infrequent reaction upon the passing of another inmate, mom observes. However, she considers the ado over this latest casualty more than peculiar. And having said that much, she resumes her reading.

She is reading aloud to me, the same paragraph from the same story as always: Slowly from comma to comma the lady of the manor is descending the spiral stairs in one serpentine sentence which coils from the top of the page down to the bottom, where it comes to a tentative halt at a semicolon. (Mom reads the punctuation with the text—a hangover from her proofreading days, I imagine.)

Maybe the footman ought to sneak up behind the great lady, grab her by the bustle and throw her down the rest of the stairs to speed up the action, I improvise.

Mom shrugs. My rewrite might amuse today's generation. But it would not have amused Mr. J.

No sense of humor. That's my mom for you. She is so serious, she even refuses to see the comical side of Miss Nobody's death.

ð

The body was discovered at lunchtime by a young nurse's aide who found Miss Nobody curled up in bed, tinier than ever in her bulky flannel robe, and with the granny glasses still on her nose as if she had just dozed off for a little nap. The nightlight was burning and a pink dildo was buzzing atop the centerfold of a well-thumbed copy of *Playboy* dating back to the sixties.

ð

The doctor signs the death certificate and delivers it to the inner office. Whereupon the director, white, of course, and a buddy of the former mayor, receives the report from the black nurse's aide. She gives him the facts, unresponsive to his winks and innuendos as he grills her for details. How much nudity was displayed on the centerfold? Which region of the human form was bared? And how did she know that the pink object she saw was a dildo? he inquires, swiveling in the leather chair behind his desk as he slowly licks his lips.

The cool young woman plays dumb, and so is dismissed with a smirk and a final wink. And now the padded door opens to admit select members of the staff for an in-depth briefing.

At the Bide-a-Wee a "fatality" is routinely minimized. No gain in reminding our guests of what's looming ahead. However, in this present case, circumstantial evidence implies such undesirable conclusions, it must be handled with the utmost care. Top secret. Classified material—agreed? Frankly, the scenario is so revolting, so damaging to our public image, we wish it would just go away.

❦

Here the doctor steps from the shadows to meddle. He has no vote. But he loves to confound the establishment. Why the hush-hush? The Bide-a-Wee image has not been tarnished. On the contrary,it has been vastly enhanced. Among the aged, any kind of sexual activity is a welcome sign of good health and should be advertised as such, not covered up. Granted, the old like the young and the restless—forgive the pun—have died during coitus or masturbation. But rarely, very rarely have they died because of it. Indeed, masturbation is easiest on the heart and thus provides an extra margin of safety for graying America.

The director is noisily shuffling papers. The doctor smiles.

Speaking of safe sex, he proceeds, fondling his stethoscope, the old are safer by far than are the young. In our society, with teenage pregnancy, AIDS and illiteracy raging, I strongly advocate a mandatory course in onanism for every first-grader.

The director gets up. He stomps out and doc sits down on the shiny, abandoned desk. Of course, our main concern is and must always be the safety of our residents, he remembers as he strokes his gray beard. Their welfare is our business, their longevity our bread and butter. Ladies and gentlemen: may I suggest that we start to distribute auto-erotic gadgets together with so-called skin magazines for those who want them regardless of sexual preference, faith or gender. Japanese high tech has developed a truly dazzling variety of finely honed instruments to stimulate the oft-neglected private parts of the elderly and afford them orgastic adventures incomparably more exciting than those engendered by old-fashioned tools, not to mention primordial activation by hand. . . .

But just as doc is warming up to his topic, the PR person, former beauty queen from Platzburg, cuts him short.

The Bide-a-Wee has no plans to convert into a sex shop, she snaps.

The doctor smiles. He slides off the desk and exits. And as the padded door falls softly shut behind him, he reaches under his overcoat and turns off the tape recorder.

❧

Of course the lid was blown off Miss Nobody's secret long before the management got wind of it. Bide-a-Weeans who yesterday didn't know a dildo from a doodle, toss and twist the word around at supper over the stewed prunes.

> *dill de dollar*
> *doll de deli*
> *doodoo die*

Miss Nobody has become somebody, a shot in the arm, and in one transient social worker's lingo "a therapeutic experience for our girls."

The male wards are less impressed. *Playboy* is old hat. Who looks at it, 'cept little boys and queer biddies?

And from a corpulent, somnolent tavern keeper to a drunken clientele of ghosts: I used to finger fuck my old lady. . . .

◈

Mom in her corner remains impervious to it all. Down on the sidewalk in the fallen leaves a child is skipping rope. A boy? A girl? A leprechaun, perhaps? Mom knocks at the window. The child looks up at her with impish eyes, swings the rope like a lasso over its head, sticks out its tongue and runs.

Has mom read *Playboy*?

I skimmed through it years ago, at the dentist's. But I recall nothing in it that I would consider risqué. If the publishers were out to sell erotica, why on earth would they print an interview with Jimmy Carter?

Mom, who is Jimmy Carter?

◈

At last I've psyched myself sufficiently to stop by mom's apartment for a final inspection. The wreckers are due tomorrow. I'm about to unlock the door when a plaintive meow from the inside freezes me to the spot. But when I turn the key, the sound is gone. The large room is an empty space without a past.

I squint against a sudden rush of light. No cats. No ghosts, only the suffocating smell of Mr.Clean. Jack has removed more than mom's few belongings. He has gotten rid of the accumulated dirt, has scoured, scrubbed, scraped, and polished the windows to a high gloss so mom will have her sun. He still hopes that the building can be saved at the eleventh hour. (He signed a petition to that effect.) It has always been his conviction that she should live out her days in her own home.

You say when and I'll move her back, he says. But would he be able to share the costs of a sleep-in nurse? Jack is a dreamer. He rarely visits mom—embarrassed or annoyed, I guess, because she might again correct his grammar. But his affection and concern for her are real.

Ъ

Not a trace of Mr.Clean in the big closet. I've stepped into a piney fragrance of long ago summers. Mom has preserved their forest magic in a cushion stuffed with balsam and spruce.

A plump, round cushion, small enough to fit into my fist.

I pick it off the top shelf, sniff it and roll it between my palms to make my hands smell sweet like mom taught me when I was little. The colors on the burlap have faded. I can barely distinguish the picture of a wild goose on the wing, and below it the lettering: CANADA.

souvenir from beautiful has worn away.

ЪЪ

Do you remember ADANAC? I ask mom.

Adanac?

CANADA in mirror writing. I talked myself to sleep repeating it: ADANAC ADANAC. . . .

Adanac?

Canada, mom. We used to take the train up there in August, when I was little. (I.e. before you shipped me off to summer camp to be tortured by smelly girl scout types and eaten alive by bugs, I'm tempted to add but I refrain.)

Remember, mom? Those long, long summers?

No response. Only a baffled look.

In ADANAC the summers never ended. I've brought them to you, all those wonderful summers in one small package.

I waft the cushion under her nose and she inhales real deep. It's coming back, she says, shutting her eyes. The dense, high forest climbing up the mountain side dark green. The lobster boats asway in the windy harbor. There was a tiny gift shop near the wharf. We bought the souvenir and missed the last mailboat.

We missed it because of me. The wind blew your hat away and I was chasing after it. That's how the boat left without us. And the hat was gone too. A huge white hat. You looked awesome in it. We watched from the wharf, how it danced on the whitecaps. But then we lost it in the storm. Some storm we had that day—remember, mommy?

I haven't called her mommy since I was little. I wish I could curl up in her lap.

Mom says she bought another hat just like the lost one. Big hats are an extravagance she can't resist. She is rolling the cushion between her hands. May she keep it?

But of course, mom. It's yours!

True, it belongs in my linen chest with the pillowslips for sweet dreams. She has dropped the cushion into her purse. I must be getting home, she says. When can I leave? Tomorrow?

I smooth her hair. I stroke her hands, thinking how soft they are, how well-formed, still; while I realize in a panic that I must tell her about the apartment. It's now or never, I think, the background noise of the inmates reverberating in my ears like an ominous chorus.

I grit my teeth. I press her hand to my burning cheek. Your building will be gone by tomorrow, I finally say, ashamed like I was the wrecker.

But the dreaded news has passed her by. I must be getting home, she repeats.

☙

ACKACKACKACK—boom—CRASH!

The sky is falling down. Mom's house is falling. The wrecking squad's infernal din shakes the foundations of the Bide-a-Wee. It catapults the sitcoms into the war zone and stirs the lifeless TV fans to action. Some clap their hands and shout hurrah. Others yell shut up and switch channels. But the hellish noise prevails.

Mom in her corner by the window is busy with a crossword puzzle. *Popular foliage plant of mint family?* Six letters. . . . The mint family. . . . Can you help?

She puts the pencil down and glances at the window from where she liked to contemplate the outside world. But the air is gritty with the debris that mushrooms from the demolition site some blocks away. Her window is covered with dust and she can't see the people on the short stretch of sidewalk, or watch the wind in the ailanthus tree.

The noise? she says. The noise will cease in time. But the dust makes me fear the worst. Once they have stolen our sun, how will our garden grow?

ੀ▲·

We are leaving the city. We'll be driving twelve hundred miles west, right into the heart of the U.S.A. I'm so happy to get away, I don't care where to or how far. The only problem is what to tell mom.

We'll have her live with us of course. That's Jack's solution. The chicken farm he's taking off his granpa's hands is small, and the house that comes with it ain't so big either. But there's always room for one more. (A typical Jack truism.)

Don't you fret. Trust me, hon. She'll have her own space and her own little flower garden. Sure, the country's on a downward slump and farmers are hurting. But granpa's managed and so will we. No rent bills! Think of it! If things get tight, we can survive on the produce. It's not a bad life and your mom won't be lonely. Granpa is a sociable old cuss. He's just too far on in years to keep running the farm by himself.

Fresh air, fresh milk, fresh eggs, fresh corn. Your mom will love it, honey.

I say she won't she never will she cannot live with us at least not yet no never.

I'm rattling off excuses to sound less heartless. Mom will be miserable in the midst of nowhere, with nothing to see except corn. Forget your grandpa. The only grandpa she can tolerate sits forever in the sundown in her head. No, it won't do. It won't be safe to move her. And if we did, we couldn't leave the kid alone with her for even a moment. Remember when we brought him to the Bide-a-Wee and let her hold him—how she overreacted? She became so emotional, she was shaking and lost her grip. Supposing we hadn't caught him in time, can you imagine what would have happened?

I'm on the verge of tears. Jack, if you love me, don't let her live with us. At least not yet. It would kill me. It will kill our marriage.

Easy, hon. No reason why we can't put her up at the local old folks home for a spell. It's not the greatest place, but it's nearby so we can have her to the house for meals and see how it works. Our farm is only a short drive from the home, on the same dirt road.

(and across from the old cemetery where his ma and pa and granma are buried. I am familiar with the layout)

Let me sleep on it, Jack. For now we'll have to keep her where she is.

(in limbo land. like me)

❧

in limbo land in
the backyard of
the old folks home
sleeps the old graveyard
no sweat to drive
into either facility
don't skid in the mud folks
mind
    that
        big
            hole

❧

Spring. And the world looks happy. The mounted cop in front of the city shelter smiles sunny and sweet from the height of his horse as a neat pile of steaming horse shit blows fantasies of pastures up my nose. I've switched my walkman from hard core rap to country music. *Just before the battle, mother. . . .* Wrong channel.

This is my last trip to the Bide-a-Wee and I feel like a convict released from jail after a long sentence. Free at last. Goodbye, I love you mom, I do. But goodbye.

Today I'll have to tell her that we are moving away. How will she react? But I've stopped eating my heart out. I haven't even decided how to package the news. I'll play it by ear.

I'm taking the shortest route. No more detours as on previous trips. No stopping by the Dairy Queen or with the disenfranchised as I've learned to think of the homeless. (Makes their problem far less personal and guilt inflicting.) No more delays!

The Bide-a-Wee is swimming toward me in swirls of light at the end of the endless street; and I sprint the last few yards, anxious to get it over with and get on with my life.

૨∙

I'm in the hallway, ready to push through the jam of wheelchairs and walkers, when I'm stopped at the desk. *All visitors except nearest kin are required to sign the guest book.* The clerk points a thumb over his shoulder at the framed document.

I am the nearest kin, I say. And I add, though he damn well knows it, that I am the daughter.

No audible reply. Only a sneer at my PRO CHOICE T-shirt. I sign. He sticks an I.D. stickum to my chest, smack over the logo, and signals me to proceed.

ॐ

Mom is not in the dining hall. In her corner an attendant is leaning out the window, whistling through his fingers at some chicks in the street. Mom must be in her room.

Rather than wait with the crowd by the elevator, I decide to climb the stairs. Only four flights, and already I'm out of breath. The smell of disinfectants makes me dizzy and I halt, then start down the snot green corridor along a row of singles, doubles and four-bed wards.

Shouts, sobs through open doors. Mumblings, sing-song moans and radio static. I compulsively gape at a shriveled man in fetus position on mussed, soiled sheets. Someone somewhere is playing the harmonica: *Good night, ladies . . .* The first four bars, over and over. A telephone rings and rings.

I glance behind me and almost collide with a gurney which is rolling by so rapidly, I don't recognize the patient, barely the doctor. In seconds they've been swallowed by the elevator, and now I race to mom's room *49* at the end of the corridor. The room is empty.

I stare at the lone geranium in bloom on the window sill. They have taken her away. I am certain. The sudden wail of an ambulance confirms my certainty, and dropping down on her bed, exhausted, I feel an odd mixture of deep sadness and utter release; and a desire to keep lying there on mom's bed and do nothing.

ॐ

Cardiac arrest in *41*. . . . change sheets for new occupant.
. . . The walkie-talkie from the corridor kicks me out of my
stupor and back on my feet. *Has anyone seen my mother?*

The floor nurse says she has not seen her since breakfast.

Why don't you inquire downstairs, dearie? Her tone is
reassuring. She says not to worry and wipes my face with a
tissue. I hadn't been aware that I was crying.

Ask downstairs at the desk. They'll locate her, she says
with an encouraging smile. They always do.

❧

Not to worry! But the administration says it without sym-
pathy; and when I suggest that they contact the missing per-
sons bureau, they turn openly hostile. They can handle the
situation. I am not to interfere. The premises are already being searched by a competent staff. The search may take a
while. This is an old building. But they will locate her. Seniors do get disoriented and may roam about the premises.
It does not happen frequently, but it can happen, and in any
case she couldn't possibly have left the building. The newly
installed high tech security gate is one hundred percent
foolproof and has been tested with spectacular success by
the prison system.

Don't meddle. We know our business. Trust us. The tight-
assed PR bitch feeds me the usual crap. You're overwrought.
Sit down and read the latest issue of *The Body Builder*. Sit
down. Relax! Relax!

I explode and hit the institution with a barrage of profani-
ties.

Shouldn't have lost my cool. From accuser I become the accused and am warned that my remarks amount to libel. The Bide-a-Wee has retained an immaculate reputation for nearly a century, and the district attorney who used to serve on our board of trustees. . . .

Shove it! I give them the finger and storm out into the noisy street.

ớ♠

I had a sudden hunch I'd find her there. It was a gut feeling and I was only mildly surprised when I saw her wheel herself leisurely against the traffic and onto the sidewalk, impervious to the cars and trucks that had come to a screeching halt.

And she was happy! I could tell from afar as she called out to me through a pandemonium of honking horns and cursing drivers. The glorious sky! The balmy breeze! The SUN!

I'm in Heaven. . . . She hums the tune and spreads out her arms to me.

I never saw her so high—elated by the weather, triumphant over her escape; bubbling over with excitement as she gives me a breathless account of her great adventure. Out there, she says, pointing across the street at a small green island, there, under those trees, she made the acquaintance of a young Puerto Rican who played the guitar for her.

An artist blessed with Segovia's divine touch and the dark gold face of a Fra Angelico saint. I sat glued to my chair while his music carried me away until I wept for joy. The city began to resonate with a mysterious light. . . .

She falls all at once silent. She shakes her head impatiently and bites her nails.

What is it, mom?

I'm embarrassed. He seemed rather down on his luck and I had every intention to pay him. But I had no money on me—not a dime. He was waiting by my chair while I went through my empty wallet, and then he quite abruptly walked away. I am so embarrassed! Do you think you could find him for me? He deserves some token of my gratitude. What do you say?

What can I say? I kiss her and fasten the scarf which is about to fly off with the breeze. She has given me the fright of my life. But I won't reproach her. I wheel her around the block at a fast clip and buy her a bunch of red tulips. One more trip around the block. Then back to the Bide-a-Wee. She does not object. She is tired.

The tulips are sliding down her lap and I catch them before they land on the sidewalk.

I had a delightful outing, she says through a long yawn, while I swear a silent oath that I will come for her and have her live with us in the country the moment we are settled. Come what may.

ᴥ

The paper boy is pedalling past, whistling as he tosses the rolled up paper to land on the roof. Let Jack climb the ladder and rescue the local rag. Me, I have a good excuse to stay put on the porch in the shade. He's got me pregnant again.

Should I tell mom?

To tell or not to tell. The pun is tough to resist. Our nearest town is Ophelia. Between mom and me stretch more than a thousand miles. But the predicament remains the same: Should I tell her?

I have to get a letter out today. She doesn't hear from me too often. But in case I let on that I'm pregnant, I may have to face what I've successfully blocked off so far: when to come for her and bring her here.

We ought to do it soon, says Jack. She's entitled to be with the family when her new grandchild is born.

Perhaps so. But what about me? What am I entitled to? No, I can't tell her, not yet. I am simply not ready. Besides, it could well be a false alarm, a false pregnancy as happened to one of our cats. A big fat tom, believe it or not. Even the vet was stunned. But granpa wasn't, he says the world's gone batty, his hens are laying poor quality eggs, too many chicks die, too many don't hatch, all of which he blames on Washington and the professors who mess with genes and the climate. We haven't seen nothing yet. There's worse in store for man and beast alike, you wait and see.

When I listen to granpa I ask myself is it wise to bring another child into this loused up, overpopulated world? Should I consider an abortion? But here in the Bible Belt abortion is a dirty word, which means it would cost us plenty. We'd have to mortgage granpa's land to pay for it.

ᐦᐧ

I start the letter as I always do: dear mom; then instantly pause and wonder: *dear mom*? The two little words reveal my duplicity. Not unlike the proverbial *dear john* letter they are a subterfuge, an excuse for excuses. Writing to her, I postpone a decision indefinitely. Why write at all? It isn't fair to either one of us. But we have to communicate, somehow.

I have phoned her. She has a phone in her room. But she rarely stays in her room. And the desk won't make much of an effort to find her. Once I was put on hold for close to an hour. And when her voice emerged at last from the background murmur, the operator in Ophelia cut us off. Nobody gives a shit.

But the phone is no solution anyway. On those few occasions when I got her on the line, she took it for granted that I was in the city—around the corner. How wonderful! Come over right away!

And when I'd interrupt to explain that I was calling long distance, her voice would suddenly be distant too.

That's quite all right. We will make it another time. . . . I'm rather tired anyway . . . so many friends came to visit. . . .

Her pretense that she hasn't been forgotten by the world is perhaps the most depressing moment of our talk, though I ought to be prepared for it from the Bide-a-Wee where such make-believe is routine. I figure that once you are over the hill, you can't admit you are lonely, else people will think that you are on your final trip afloat on the arctic ice, without the blessings of an Eskimo chant. And the world will give up on you.

≈

Scrap the phone call. Pull yourself together and write your mom. Can I make it a postcard? O no you can't. Quit stalling and move your ass.

I move it, from the porch swing back to the table from where I stare at the blank page, then out at the silver horizon beyond waves of ripening corn. The empty swing creaks in its hinges like an old schooner and I wish myself aboard the schooner and am ready to sail the high seas.

Hi, mom! I've switched to a different greeting. The casual touch does the trick. Hi, shoulda written ages ago but haven't had one single quiet moment.

I'm over the hump and continue without further scruples. Your dutiful facile-pen daughter, that's little Miss Me. Once I kick start myself, there's no stopping me. I zoom along, busy to prove how busy I am with yard work and house work and mouse work and seven cats. (Scratch the cats. They touch a raw nerve. Replace them with our three dogs.)

The dogs are barking. In no time I've covered page 1 with half truths, idiotic gossip from Ophelia, downright lies and dumb evasions. The kid's doing fine in nursery school. That's all I dare say of our son, afraid I'd trip myself and tell her I'm pregnant. Deep down I know I want her to know.

Page 2. The ballpoint is wearing thin. The writing looks pale. I'm about to paint a discouraging picture of the surroundings—awful climate, lousy transportation—when I'm suddenly off on a different tangent. Dear mom, I may not always act on it but I love you very much.

An automatic reflex? The ink is barely visible. But I write on. Dear mom, I've been doing a lot of thinking. Out here in zeroville there isn't much else I can do. I've been thinking over that spring day, my wheeling you from your freedom ride back to the Bide-a-Wee where I told you about our move to the farm and gave you my promise that we would come for you and have you live with us as soon as we had settled down.

You didn't respond and I thought you hadn't understood me right. So I said loud and clear, cross my heart, mom, we want to take you in.

You still said nothing. I was arranging the tulips in an empty milk carton. You were watching my every move. A garbage truck was rattling past outside and you waited for the noise to subside.

Take me in? you said at last. It seems to me that I have been taken in by you for a long time.

Mom, I felt terribly hurt. I really had sworn to myself that I would never break my promise. But of course I was fooling myself and you caught on fast. You made that abundantly clear. My promise was a bad check.

&

What can I say? Often when I think of you I might be holding a twice exposed slide against the lamp. You are in the sun on the porch swing, a younger mom. You are at the Bide-a-Wee in your chair in the shadows.

Believe me, I'm not faking when I put you off month after month. Rather I'm hoping to pacify you the way I do when I shove a lollipop into the kid's mouth to keep him from screaming my ears off. . . .

An act of self-defense? I don't have the answers. I only know that I do love you, mom. But there's no justice, just like I heard you say so many times when I was a kid.

&

Some of this I get on paper. But most I write in my head.

&

No justice? I rather doubt that I would ever make such a blanket statement, I hear mom say as I imagine her in her old place by the window. She folds the letter and stuffs it back into the envelope which is stained with breakfast coffee.

Good news from your folks? a nurse's aide asks in passing.

The usual. . . . My daughter urges me to live with them. . . .

Mom's enunciation is precise. Her gray eyes are blurred as she gazes into space.

However, I have my reservations, she says to no one. Their residence is so remote. . . .

I've torn up the letter and follow the paper flakes sail on the wind to the fields of ripening corn. Perhaps I will write a postcard. The only picture postcard I could find shows Ophelia's courthouse frozen in a raspberry sunset. Local color. But no beauty. Still. . . .

> dear mom
> miss you
> want to
> see you
>   love
>   me
> p.s. i'm pregnant mommy

Born in Strasbourg in Alsace-Lorraine (claimed at various times by Germany and France), Marianne Hauser attended a strict French lycée; outraged by a principal's tirade against The Weimar Republic, she spoke out and was expelled. Her mother enrolled her in a peace-oriented institution, and Hauser went on to the University of Berlin, skipping, she reports, most of her law classes.

However, she attended courses on Provençal literature, Etruscan art, and Oceanic masks, and began writing stories. She married as the German Republic began to crumble, and was living on the island of Capri when the Nazis torched the Reichstag. At 22 she traveled to Paris, divorced and out of work, and finished her first novel while surviving by writing interviews, fashion reports, and other journalistic pieces. After reading Céline's *Voyage au bout de la nuit,* she decided to travel to Asia, reporting her experiences as she went. The Basle, Switzerland paper *Basler National Zeitung* agreed to take a chance on the project, and supported her travels through India, Malaysia, Cambodia, Ceylon, Siam, China, Manchuria, Formosa, Japan, and lastly, the USA.

In Hawaii she finished her first novel *Indisches Gaukelspiel* (Indian Phantom Play), based on her Indian experiences, which was published by Vienna's Zinnen Verlag. From Honolulu, she sailed on a Japanese freighter to San Francisco, a world, she reports, which was more exotic and confusing to her than all the others.

Pleased by her journalistic travel pieces, the editor asked her to return to the United States to report on politics. She lived for while near Columbia University, cutting her links with Europe, and reviewed for *The New Republic, New York Times, Herald Tribune,* and *Saturday Review of Literature.* With the encouragement of Coby Gilman, editor of *Travel* magazine, she began writing her first American novel, *Dark Dominion,* which was published in 1947 by Random House.

In the early 1940s she married concert pianist Michael Kirchberger, and upon his release from the army, moved with him to Greensboro, North Carolina and Kirksville, Missouri; and during these years she published the novels *The Choir Invisible* and *Prince Ishmael* (Sun & Moon Classic: 4) and completed the collection of stories, *A Lesson in Music*.

Upon her divorce in 1966, Hauser returned to New York City, and,on a trip to Paris, wrote *The Talking Room*. Sun & Moon Press published **her** novel, *The Memoirs of the Late Mr. Ashley: An American Comedy* in 1986.

SUN & MOON CLASSICS

The Sun & Moon Classics is a publicly supported, nonprofit program to publish new editions, translations, or republications of outstanding world literature of the late nineteenth and twentieth centuries. Through its publication of living authors as well as great masters of the century, the series attempts to redefine what usually is meant by the idea of a "classic" by dehistorizing the concept and embracing a new, ever changing literary canon.

Organized by the Contemporary Arts Educational Project, Inc., a nonprofit corporation, and published by its program Sun & Moon Press, the series is made possible, in part, by grants and individual contributions.

This book was made possible, in part, through matching grants from the National Endowment for the Arts and from the California Arts Council, through an organizational grant from the Andrew W. Mellon Foundation, through a grant for advertising and promotion from the Lila Wallace/Reader's Digest Fund, and through contributions from the following individuals:

Charles Altieri (Seattle, Washington)
John Arden (Galway, Ireland)
Jesse Huntley Ausubel (New York, New York)
Dennis Barone (West Hartford, Connecticut)
Jonathan Baumbach (Brooklyn, New York)
Guy Bennett (Los Angeles, California)
Bill Berkson (Bolinas, California)
Steve Benson (Berkeley, California)
Charles Bernstein and Susan Bee (New York, New York)
Sherry Bernstein (New York, New York)
Dorothy Bilik (Silver Spring, Maryland)
Bill Corbett (Boston, Massachusetts)
Fielding Dawson (New York, New York)
Robert Crosson (Los Angeles, California)
Tina Darragh and P. Inman (Greenbelt, Maryland)
David Detrich (Los Angeles, California)
Christopher Dewdney (Toronto, Canada)

Philip Dunne (Malibu, California)
George Economou (Norman, Oklahoma)
Elaine Equi and Jerome Sala (New York, New York)
Lawrence Ferlinghetti (San Francisco, California)
Richard Foreman (New York, New York)
Howard N. Fox (Los Angeles, California)
Jerry Fox (Aventura, Florida)
In Memoriam: Rose Fox
Melvyn Freilicher (San Diego, California)
Miro Gavran (Zagreb, Croatia)
Peter Glassgold (Brooklyn, New York)
Barbara Guest (New York, New York)
Perla and Amiram V. Karney (Bel Air, California)
Fred Haines (Los Angeles, California)
Fanny Howe (La Jolla, California)
Harold Jaffe (San Diego, California)
Ira S. Jaffe (Albuquerque, New Mexico)
Alex Katz (New York, New York)
Tom LaFarge (New York, New York)
Mary Jane Lafferty (Los Angeles, California)
Michael Lally (Santa Monica, California)
Norman Lavers (Jonesboro, Arkansas)
Jerome Lawrence (Malibu, California)
Stacey Levine (Seattle, Washington)
Herbert Lust (Greenwich, Connecticut)
Norman MacAffee (New York, New York)
Rosemary Macchiavelli (Washington, DC)
Martin Nakell (Los Angeles, California)
Toby Olson (Philadelphia, Pennsylvania)
Maggie O'Sullivan (Hebden Bridge, England)
Rochelle Owens (Norman, Oklahoma)
Marjorie and Joseph Perloff (Pacific Palisades, California)
Dennis Phillips (Los Angeles, California)
David Reed (New York, New York)
Ishmael Reed (Oakland, California)
Janet Rodney (Santa Fe, New Mexico)
Joe Ross (Washington, DC)
Dr. Marvin and Ruth Sackner (Miami Beach, Florida)
Floyd Salas (Berkeley, California)
Tom Savage (New York, New York)
Leslie Scalapino (Oakland, California)
James Sherry (New York, New York)
Aaron Shurin (San Francisco, California)
Charles Simic (Strafford, New Hampshire)

If you would like to be a contributor to this series, please send your tax-deductible contribution to The Contemporary Arts Educational Project, Inc., a non-profit corporation, 6026 Wilshire Boulevard, Los Angeles, California 90036

*First Publication
**Revised Edition